THORFINN THE NICEST VIKING

To Jessica – D.M.

To Eben and Aurelie, the little Vikings – R.M.

Young Kelpies is an imprint of Floris Books
First published in 2015 by Floris Books

Text © 2015 David MacPhail. Illustrations © 2015 Floris Books
David MacPhail and Richard Morgan have asserted their rights
under the Copyright, Designs and Patent Act 1988 to
be identified as the Author and Illustrator of this work

The publisher acknowledges subsidy from
Creative Scotland towards the publication
of this volume

 This book is also
available as an eBook

British Library CIP data available
ISBN 978-178250-159-6
Printed in Great Britain
by Bell & Bain Ltd

Thorfinn
and the
Gruesome Games

written by David Macphail
illustrated by Richard Morgan

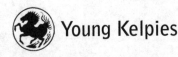 Young Kelpies

OSWALD
WISE MAN OF INDGAR

VELDA

HAGAR THE
THUNDER-BELLY

LOGRID THE
LIMB-SPLITTER

INDGAR VILLAGE

COW SHEDS

OSWALD'S HOUSE

THE GREAT HALL

THORFINN'S HOUSE

MARKET PLACE

CHAPTER 1

Indgar was like any normal Viking village, with sword fighting in the morning, wrestling in the afternoon, and at least three big punch-ups before dinner. And that was just for the old folk.

Around lunchtime the women of the village gathered round the well with their laundry. Not that they ever did any laundry. Usually they just catapulted it into the fjord. It would almost always wash up on shore the next day, slightly cleaner than it had been when it went in.

One of the women spotted the chief's son – a
boy called Thorfinn – stepping out from behind a
large sheet covering the great hall.

"What are you up to, Thorfinn?" she asked.

"Good day, dear ladies," said Thorfinn, removing
his helmet. "You'll be the first to see my new
surprise. Ta da!" He pulled the sheet away.
The women's screams could be
heard on the other side of the village.

Thorfinn's father, Harald the Skull-
Splitter, Chief of Indgar, sat alone
in his chamber, wrapped in furs.
He was writing down a list of the

village's competitors for this year's International Gruesome Games. It did not make good reading. The only contest they had a chance of winning was belching.

Harald scratched his head and looked around his private chamber. The walls were adorned with stags' heads, trophies and souvenirs from his many adventures. Harald eyed the village's ceremonial sword, Whirlwind. He had carried it into battle many times. It was a symbol of his power as village chief.

His eyes moved slowly to the empty space next to it, where his ceremonial shield, Sword-Blunter, used to sit. Whirlwind and Sword-Blunter belonged together, but the shield had been lost in battle many years ago. The chief of the neighbouring village, Magnus the Bone-Breaker, had it now.

Magnus would be at the games too, thought Harald. He would be gloating over the shield and showing it off to everyone. Harald would do anything to get it back.

Suddenly, half the men of the village stormed into his house, yelling over each other and trying to get through his chamber door.

"CHIEF!"

"BOSS!"

Their faces pressed together as they all became

stuck, their eyes bulging out of their heads, their

arms sticking out all over the place.

"EEK!"
"HUUYYYY! BOSS, LISTEN!"
"BLEUUUUGH! CHIEF, QUICK!"

Harald did not like to be interrupted. He rose from his seat, glaring at the men with venom. Harald was famous for his incredibly twitchy eye. It could strike fear into the heart of anyone, even the fiercest of the fierce. And it was quite useful at times like this.

He deployed the twitch. The men froze in the doorway, terrified.

"WHAT is the meaning of this?" Harald roared. "Barging into my house, my own private chamber. Well, what do you have to say for yourselves, you fish-faced idiots?"

For a moment nobody spoke. Lots of eyes just looked round at one another. Then, it was as if a spring had been released, as the men exploded through the door and fell in a heap at Harald's feet.

"S-s-sorry, Chief," said one of them sheepishly. "B-b-but it's your son, Thorfinn."

"He's gone too far this time," said another.

"You've got to stop him," said one more.

Harald sank into his throne, his head in his hands.

"Ugh!" he sighed. "What has that boy of mine been up to now?"

CHAPTER 2

Harald marched down to the marketplace, leading his men.

"Look," they told him, "we know Thorfinn is clever and has saved the village many times. But we can't put up with his behaviour any more."

Harald dreaded to think what he was going to find. This morning he had asked Thorfinn to tidy up the market place and clean out the cowshed. Two simple jobs. What could have gone wrong?

An angry crowd had gathered outside the great hall. They were led by Erik the Ear-Masher, Harald's second in command. He had only one eye (the other was covered by an eye patch) and a face like a bashed cauliflower. The two of them fought often, and it looked like he was in the mood for another fight right now.

The crowd was standing in a circle looking on in horror at Thorfinn.

Erik bounded up towards Harald. "Look! Look what that son of yours has done to our horrible, unwelcoming village!"

Harald saw what they were angry about right away.

Thorfinn had painted the great hall a new colour – bright purple.

Harald was a man who knew very little fear. He'd fought the ferocious Vandals of Valhalla Island, the cannibal Cossacks of Minsk, and even the One-eyed Warrior Monks of Lindisfarne, and none of them had truly scared him. But now he was scared. If other Vikings saw this, the village would never live it down.

"PURPLE!" he cried. "PURPLE! You painted our hall PURPLE?"

"Good day, dear Father," said Thorfinn, whose

pet pigeon, Percy, was perched on his hand. "I just thought it would brighten the place up a bit."

"PURPLE? PURPLE!"

"Actually, it's more like mauve," said one of the villagers.

"No," said another. "There's more of a reddish hue if you ask me."

"You're both wrong. That's magenta," said a third.

"No, orchid!"

"That's mulberry, you idiot!"

"ENOUGH!" cried Harald in his hugest, boomiest voice. "Vikings DO NOT have arguments about colour schemes." He turned to Thorfinn. "And Viking villages DO NOT have purple walls. Do you understand? Now, repaint the hall."

"Of course, Father," said Thorfinn. "I'll do anything to help. But what colour should I paint it?"

"What do you mean, boy?!" Harald was spitting with rage. "Paint it back to the colour it was before."

"You mean, mud?"

"Yes. Mud," said Harald. "I mean, what's wrong with mud as a colour anyway?"

The Vikings all agreed that mud was the colour

for them. They hastily arranged a work party, who smeared armfuls of wet mud all over the walls.

"But that's not all," said Erik. "Come and look at this!"

He and the other villagers led Harald to the entrance of the village. Harald wondered what new horror would await him there.

A stretch of hillside next to the village had been dug over and replanted with lots of tiny flowers. They were arranged in huge letters to read:

Harald clasped his hand to his mouth. He trembled with fear and rage. The rest of the villagers started wailing like they were at a funeral.

"Thorfinn, THORFINN! What is the meaning of this outrage?"

"Father dear," said Thorfinn, appearing at his side, "I've entered the village in the 'Norway in Bloom' competition this year."

"Norway in Bloom!" Harald croaked. "Get this through your skull – Vikings don't enter flower competitions. And Vikings don't put out welcome signs. We're ruthless barbarians. We HATE visitors."

"Yes," the villagers echoed. "Death to all visitors!"

"Except my Auntie Madge," said one.

"And Bert the oil salesman," said another.

"And the travelling druid of Oslo," said a third.

Harald unleashed his twitchy eye on them to shut them up.

"Oh yes," said Thorfinn, rubbing his chin. "I keep forgetting that bit about being ruthless barbarians."

Harald sighed. He knew Thorfinn would never understand. Besides, one glance at his son's mild, well-meaning eyes was enough to drain the anger from anyone – even he, a man who was known across Europe as 'The Terror of the North Sea'.

"Come with me, son. We need to have a little talk."

"Of course, my dear old dad," said Thorfinn.

Harald put his arm round his son and led him away from the angry crowd.

Behind them, yet another work party was frantically rearranging Thorfinn's flower display.

Now it read, in big bold letters:

CHAPTER 3

Harald slumped on a rock and plonked Thorfinn upon his knee.

"Look, boy, tomorrow we set sail for Uraig for this year's Gruesome Games."

Uraig was a distant island in the Scottish sea where the annual games were always held.

"I know," said Thorfinn, "and I'm very much looking forward to it."

"You're the smartest of us all, so we couldn't go without you. But you must try to fit in. Do you understand?"

"Of course," said Thorfinn. "I'll certainly try anything for you, Father."

"I know you will," said Harald, though he wondered if Thorfinn could ever be different. Like any Viking man, all Harald had ever wanted for a son was a normal, ferocious barbarian thug. Someone he could teach in the ways of pillaging, plundering and burning stuff to the ground. Somehow Harald had ended up with the nicest, most polite boy who'd ever lived. A boy who'd earned himself the name: Thorfinn the Very-Very-Nice-Indeed. A boy whose idea of a good time was baking scones, who went round the village doffing his helmet to everyone and saying, "Good day." It was no sort of behaviour for a Viking, never mind a chief's son.

Suddenly another voice spoke from behind a woodpile.

"I might be able to help with that."

It was Thorfinn's friend, Velda – a skinny girl with curly hair, trailing a massive axe behind her.

"What you need is someone to turn him into a good Viking, bring out his inner fury," she said, leaning

29

up against the woodpile and folding her arms. "Let me become Thorfinn's anger coach."

Harald laughed. He'd been trying to turn Thorfinn into a good Viking for years and failed miserably. He doubted this tiny girl could do better.

"Don't believe me? Watch this." She suddenly screamed. It was a scream so loud and terrifying it could wake the hounds of Helheim. She picked up her axe and swung it against the trunk of a small tree. The axe split the tree neatly in half. The top half came crashing down next to them, throwing up a cloud of dust and blowing off their helmets.

"I bet you didn't think I could get that angry, eh!"

She wasn't wrong. Harald was amazed by the fierceness of this small girl, but he still doubted that

she could help. "Yes, but how are you going to coax that sort of anger out of Thorfinn?"

Velda tested the blade of her axe with her finger. "I'd never reveal my tricks to a customer."

Harald laughed again. "Maybe that's because you don't have any tricks."

"Maybe I do," she replied. "And maybe you don't have any choice."

Harald stroked his beard. What did he have to lose?

"Okay, you have a deal," he said.

"Good." Velda spat into her hand and stretched it towards Harald's massive paw. "Of course, it means I'll have to come with you to the Gruesome Games," she said.

Aha, thought Harald, here was the real reason for

all this. Velda was determined to go to sea to find her father, Gunga the Navigator. He was the worst navigator in the history of the Vikings. He once got lost just trying to find his way out of the fjord. One day he left to seek a mystical land across the great ocean and was never seen again.

"It will never be allowed," said Harald. The other

Vikings thought her family was cursed, and girls didn't usually go on Viking voyages.

Velda leaned back against the woodpile and drummed her fingers on her chin. "Hmmm. Let me ask you a question. What's it like having Thorfinn meet other Vikings? Or, even worse, non-Vikings? Because I can stop him embarrassing you."

Harald thought about all the embarrassment Thorfinn had caused, and how much more he was capable of, and it sent a shiver up his spine.

"But how is that even possible?" cried Harald.

"I'll shadow Thorfinn everywhere," said Velda to Harald. "I'll stop him being nice and polite. Watch this!" She turned to Thorfinn again. "Thorfinn, stand up. We're going to try some role playing."

"Oh, great," said Thorfinn. "I do love pretending. What role am I playing?"

"You are playing yourself."

"Oh, I rather thought I might play someone else, but never mind."

"And you, Chief," she turned back to Harald. "You are a Viking chief."

"But I AM a Viking chief."

"I know. Another Viking chief, I mean, not you."

"And who do you get to play?" asked Thorfinn.

"I'm me."

"Right," said Thorfinn. "So we're all just being ourselves."

"Role playing is rubbish!" said Harald.

"Now shoosh!" Velda said. "Imagine we're at the

games. You bump into Thorfinn here, who you've never seen before. Say something."

"What?" said Harald. "Oh, er, you there. What's your name?"

Thorfinn's hand reached up to his helmet. He was about to take it off. His mouth opened. He was about to utter those words Harald hated to hear: "Good day, dear sir." When suddenly Velda jumped on Thorfinn's back and clasped her hand firmly over his mouth. The look on her face was deadly serious as she replied, "My friend, sir, cannot speak his name, for if he did it would strike such terror into your heart you would surely DROP DEAD!"

Harald almost fell over. He applauded. "Brilliant!"

The girl might be cursed, but she was coming with them.

CHAPTER 4

That night, a farewell feast was held in the newly-painted-and-then-splattered-with-mud-again great hall.

Erik was rabble-rousing. "Thorfinn will show us all up! Why are we taking him with us? We should leave him at home."

Harald leapt up onto the table and snarled. "You dog! You snake! You worm! We need Thorfinn and you know it. He's coming with us, and that's that." Harald whipped out his sword and chopped the head off a roast hog to make his point.

Meanwhile, in the corner by the hearth, Oswald, the wise man of the village, was telling stories about the Gruesome Games. All the children were gathered around him.

"Tell us about the Gruesome Games, Oswald!" they asked. "What's the most dangerous contest?"

Oswald stroked his long, white beard. His voice was incredibly loud and whiny. "Hmm, well, without doubt that would have to be the spear tickling."

"Spear tickling?" They laughed. "But that sounds funny, not dangerous."

"Unless what you are tickling is a hungry mountain lion."

"Tell us another story," asked the children.

"I could tell you the story of the Great Sword Fight," said Oswald.

"Oh, yes, sword fights!" said Velda.

"You see, if the Gruesome Games ends in a draw, they hold a duel between the champions of the two teams. The winner is declared the Champion of the Games.

"Many years ago there was a sword fight between Oga, a Pictish knight, and Macduff, a Scottish prince. But Macduff took ill and couldn't fight. So an unknown knight took his place.

"The two men faced each other on the field, clad

in armour and iron helmets. The fight lasted all day. They duelled like tigers all over the island, up hills and across sea cliffs. The crowd followed them, placing bets and cheering them on."

"Who won?" cried the children. "Who won?!"

"Finally Oga the Pict tumbled off a rock and broke his sword arm, and the unknown Scottish knight won. When he was offered the trophy of the games, the Great Hammer, he took off his helmet and revealed who he really was: a humble sailor called McGill. 'I am not the nobleman you think I am,' said he, 'so I can't accept this prize.'

"In those days the penalty for a commoner pretending to be a knight was to be buried up to his neck in sand while the tide was out. And that's what they did to him."

"Did he die?" cried the children eagerly.

"No, he didn't," replied Oswald. "For as dusk fell and the tide crept in, his defeated foe, Oga the Pict, dug him up. The two of them lived as brothers thereafter, fighting side by side, the Scot and the Pict."

Everyone cheered Oswald's excellent story.

✳ ✳ ✳

Afterwards, Velda turned to Thorfinn. "Does nothing make you angry?" she asked.

"Why of course, old friend," replied Thorfinn. "I remember once, when an important chieftain visited the village, my dear pet pigeon, Percy, flew into the air and pooed on the man's head. I was pretty angry that day, let me tell you."

"I remember. I was there with you. All you did was tell Percy he was a naughty bird."

"Well exactly," said Thorfinn.

"And then you fed him some nuts."

"I was, well, perhaps not so much angry as a bit peeved."

"Thorfinn, that's not anger!" said Velda. "How about if I do this?" She pinched Thorfinn's nose.

Thorfinn twiddled his nose for a bit, then sneezed. "Thanks, dear friend. I needed that. You unblocked my nose for me."

Then Velda prodded Thorfinn in the ribs. "How about that?"

"Oooh stop it!" Thorfinn laughed.

Then Velda yelled in his face. "RAAAARGH!"

Thorfinn merely looked at her and smiled. "You're funny."

Velda sat back and stroked her chin. "Hmmm. I'll find a way to bring out your anger."

At this point Oswald leaned over and said as quietly as he could (he sounded like a horse with something stuck in its teeth), "Heed my warning. You'll never change Thorfinn."

Velda might have listened to the old man's wise words, except his eyesight was so terrible, he'd leaned over in the wrong direction and was talking to a pillar.

CHAPTER 5

They left at dawn the next morning. The whole village turned out on the pier to bid them goodbye.

"Farewell!" cried Velda, waving with both hands. "We'll bring you back the Great Hammer!"

Erik the Ear-Masher, Harald's second in command, sneered with laughter. "Little girl, we have never won the Great Hammer. I mean, just look at our team."

Standing guard over a barrel of oysters was Hagar the Thunder-Belly, their belching champion. He was large and round and rosy-cheeked, with lots of red-haired pigtails poking out from under his helmet. "No one's to eat these, do you hear? They are for my training."

He delved his hand into the barrel and pulled out a clump of oyster shells, broke them open and started popping oysters into his mouth. Hagar stood with his legs apart. He took a couple of deep breaths and then erupted:

"BLLLAAAAAAARRRRRRPPPPP!"

It was the most colossal belch any of them had ever heard. It rattled their eardrums, and echoed off the mountains that rose up from either side of the fjord. It even seemed to billow the sails a bit. The whole crew applauded.

Then there was Logrid the Limb-Splitter, the village axe-throwing champion. He was tall and skinny, with a thin, wispy beard and a wizened face.

"He's good, but he's not quite good enough to win," said Erik.

"Rubbish!" said Velda, who thought Logrid was brilliant. "What do you know about axe throwing anyway, you great pudding?"

Logrid was already practising with a target board. He raised his shiny axe to his lips and kissed the blade. "Now then, Helga, let's see how the sea affects my aim." Vikings liked to give their weapons names sometimes.

With that, Logrid unleashed his axe, hitting the bull's-eye almost dead centre.

"He's possibly my biggest hero in the world," said Velda. Logrid bowed.

"Why in the name of
Thor are we taking this
small girl anyway?" said
Erik, picking Velda up like
she was a bag of turnips.
"Her father was a jinx. Every
ship he ever sailed on got
lost or sunk." Erik dangled

her over the side. "We should get rid of her."

Harald brought his fist crashing down on Erik's
helmet. The noise was like someone sounding a
huge gong across the fjord. "Put her down, you
villainous weasel!"

"Arrr! Alright, I was only joking," said Erik,
dropping Velda back onto the deck.

Then there was Floki the Sea-Urchin, their swimming champion. He was a tiny man with broad, powerful shoulders. He was staring into the distance from the prow of the ship, his face proud and serious. Floki pointed at the distant horizon straight ahead of them. "My destiny lies there, and my destiny is to win this competition."

Oswald jabbed him on the shoulder with his stick, then pointed in the other direction. "The island of Uraig lies that way, you imbecile."

As they neared the end of the fjord another ship

appeared at their side.

"It's Magnus the Bone-Breaker!" someone cried.

Harald growled and gripped his sword. He stepped up to the prow and glared across at the other boat.

Sure enough, the neighbouring village chief was standing at the helm of his ship. His gigantic son, Osric the Brick-Swallower, stood beside him. Osric was so gigantic that Magnus was using him as a sunshade.

Magnus yelled at his son, "Move to the left, the sun's in my eyes!"

"Oh, alright," replied the youth, who looked miserable.

Thorfinn waved at him. "Cheer up, my friend! We're all going on holiday."

Magnus was wearing Harald's shield and gloating, as he always did. He shouted over at them, "Hey, you lot! Fancy a race?"

"A race?" Harald bristled.

"Yes, just to the end of the fjord. First one to the open sea wins."

Harald glowered at the other chief. "Ha! We can beat you any day, you thieving swine!" He barked at the crew, "Okay, you pig-dogs, oars at the double!"

When Harald's ship was a few lengths ahead, Magnus cupped his hands and shouted over at them. "Hey, watch this." He turned to his crew. "Men, double the oars and release the turbo sail!"

A second set of oars thrust through portholes on the sides of the ship. A giant new topsail unfurled. Before they knew it Magnus's boat was beginning to draw ahead. He waved at them from the back of his ship.

"See you at Uraig Island, losers!"

"Hmm... what an interesting character," said Thorfinn.

Harald was seething with rage. "Oh, I'll get my shield back, you big cheat. Just you wait. I'll get it back, oh yes!"

CHAPTER 6

They left the fjord and turned southwest. Thorfinn
and Velda passed the time by watching the
competitors train. Logrid practised his swing, and
nearly lopped off several of the crew's ears in
the process. Floki did a lot of press-ups to keep
his shoulder muscles toned. Meanwhile, Hagar's
belching was attracting seals, who seemed to think
he was their new leader.

"Right!" Velda said suddenly, rolling up her
sleeves. "Time to get down to business." She stood
back against the rail and looked at Thorfinn.

"Be a pal and pick up my axe for me, eh?" It was only lying a few feet away from her. "It's just that my back is a bit sore."

Thorfinn smiled. "But of course. Anything for a friend."

As Thorfinn passed her, Velda stuck out her foot and tripped him up. Percy squawked and took flight as Thorfinn tumbled to the ground. The bird perched on the mast, glaring at Velda.

"I do apologise," said Thorfinn. "I seem to have stumbled. Let me just get that axe for you."

"APOLOGISE?!" Velda exploded. "What kind of a person says sorry to someone who trips them up?"

"It doesn't do to think the worst of people, especially such a good friend as you. I expect it was my fault for stumbling over your feet."

"Look, I'm telling you I tripped you up!" cried Velda.

"You're just trying to make me feel better, which is soooo like you," replied Thorfinn.

Velda flushed and smiled. "Yes, it is soooo like me, isn't it?" She checked herself. "Wait! NO! Aren't you angry?" But it was Velda who was getting angry. "I trip you up, and YOU apologise to ME?"

Thorfinn started laughing, which made Velda even angrier. "And now you're LAUGHING?! What's so funny?"

Harald was on his way past with his fishing rod. He poked Velda's arm. "You're supposed to be making Thorfinn angry, not the other way around!"

Velda took a deep breath and calmed herself. "OK, lets try this another way. C'mere Thorfinn."

Thorfinn stepped towards her. Velda dodged to one side, grabbed Thorfinn, and then pushed him over the side. He tumbled silently into the water.

"Ha! Howzat!" she cried. "I'll bet you're angry now. Thorfinn? Thorfinn??"

Thorfinn disappeared under the water. Velda suddenly felt guilty. "What have I done?"

She tugged off her boots and was about to dive in after him, when all of a sudden he resurfaced, leaping like a graceful porpoise out of the waves. He playfully spat a big stream of water out of his mouth.

"What a terrific idea, old friend!" he cried. "The water is perfect for swimming. Come on in!" Then he began doing backstroke, while Percy had a bath beside him.

"I don't believe it!" said Velda.

"That looks like a laugh!" said one of the other Vikings. "Let's all jump in!"

Before long, just about everybody was in the sea, splashing around and laughing. Velda shrugged and jumped in after them.

"What a lark!" said Thorfinn.

"You're mad!" said Velda. "Why do you have to turn every bad thing into something nice?"

"Oh, I believe in making great things out of whatever comes my way," he replied.

CHAPTER 7

On the fourth morning of their long voyage, the Vikings woke to calm seas and warm summer sun. A low-lying island appeared on the horizon.

"That's Uraig," said Oswald the wise man.

Thorfinn and Velda climbed the mast to get a good look. The Scottish island was green and treeless. They entered a rocky cove filled with other longships, and tied up alongside Magnus's ship.

Oswald demanded to be carried off the boat.

"Ach! You can walk!" cried the crew.

"Don't you realise how old I am?" whined Oswald.

"Besides, my bunions are itchy."
One of the crew reluctantly
agreed and hoisted the old
man onto his shoulders.

"Watch it, you great
haddock!" cried Oswald,
hitting the man with his stick.
The pier was a hive of Viking
activity. There were sword fighters
and wrestlers and archers all eyeing
each other up like vultures.

"There must be a dozen different Viking tribes
here," said Velda.

They were met by a tall, stern man with a bald
head, who was wearing a long purple gown.

"Greetings. My name is Sir Fergus and I am the steward of these games."

Thorfinn was about to take off his helmet and say, "Good day." Velda leapt onto his back and clasped her hands over his mouth to stop him.

"Sorry, Sir Fergus, but my friend here cannot speak his name, for if he did it would strike such terror into your heart you would surely DROP DEAD!" she said.

Sir Fergus studied Thorfinn closely for a moment. Some of the other Vikings nearby overheard, and they too turned their heads to study the boy.

"Phew! Good work," whispered Harald to Velda.

"Follow me. I will take you to your camp," said Sir Fergus. He led them up some steps through a cleft in the cliff to a large field, which was bounded on three sides by sea cliffs and on one side by a stockade. There were lines and lines of large tents, with a section for each Viking tribe.

Thorfinn and Velda burst into their tent, excited. Oswald fell through the door behind them.

"I'm bagging the top bunk," he cried.

"That's not fair," cried Velda.

"I called it first. If you aren't fast you're last," replied the old man.

"But you can hardly even walk, never mind climb up to the top bunk," said Velda.

"Well, I for one am happy to help, old friend," said Thorfinn.

Thorfinn and Velda tried as hard as they could, but they couldn't push the old man up.

"I'll go and ask for help," said Thorfinn.

Thorfinn returned with three strong men, who sighed and raised their eyes to the sky.

"You never told us it

67

was this old windbag we were helping."

They all pushed together and when Oswald was finally up, he said, "I forgot, I need to go to the toilet!" And demanded to be taken down again.

Outside, the cooks were setting up a fire and getting ready to make dinner.

"Come with me," said Oswald after he finally emerged from the toilet. Thorfinn and Velda followed him over to the wooden stockade. A staircase led up to a watchtower. "Up!" he cried, and they had to shove him up yet another staircase.

At the top,
the view opened
out across the whole
island. In the middle was
a vast green plain. There
were four other stockades at
different ends of the island. "One
for us," said Oswald. "One for the
Angles, one for the Britons, one for the
Scots and one for the Picts. All the tribes
of the west are here for the games."

"But why are we all fenced off?" asked Thorfinn.

"These people are always at each other's
throats. It has been that way for hundreds of years.
You never know when a battle is going to erupt."

In the centre of the island stood a great wooden fort on a rocky outcrop. To its left was a giant flat field surrounded by stripy tents. "That is the field where most of the competitions take place. And look there, in the middle."

In the very centre of this field was a raised bank, on which stood a giant gleaming hammer. "That is the prize we all seek: the Great Hammer itself."

CHAPTER 8

That evening they ate around the campfire. Oswald
paid a group of touring actors to perform a play for
them.

"I'm terribly excited," said Thorfinn, as they all
settled down around a makeshift stage. "I've never
seen real actors before."

The other Vikings were excited too, but for
different reasons. "Great! Will there be sword
fighting in it?" They rubbed their hands with glee.

"Yes, something with lots of battles and gory
deaths!"

The actors seemed to have other ideas though, as the play was a love story.

"BOOOO! Rubbish! Gerroff!" cried the deeply disappointed Vikings.

Thorfinn was the only one who enjoyed it. In fact, he clapped the whole way through, shouting, "Bravo!"

The Vikings started throwing food at the stage. The actors were used to being pelted with fruit and

eggs, but the Vikings threw a full salmon, a wheel of cheese and the entire roast hindquarters of an elk.

"They're an enthusiastic bunch," said Thorfinn of his fellow Vikings.

The play was wisely cut short when some of the audience members were spotted wheeling forward a military catapult and loading it with boiled reindeer heads.

"What a pity," said Thorfinn, as the actors fled the stage in terror. "Aren't actors amazing? I'd love to be able to do that."

Velda thought about that, scratching her chin. "Hmmm. Very interesting indeed."

Magnus the Bone-Breaker appeared by the campfire, carrying Harald's shiny gold shield, Sword-Blunter, on his back. His glum giant of a son, Osric the Brick-Swallower, hung at his shoulder.

Harald crackled and spat like the fire they were standing round. "What do you want here, Bone-Breaker?"

"Well, that's nice, isn't it?" replied Magnus. "I just wanted to wish you good luck, that's all. Oh, and if you're interested, to offer you the chance to win your shield back."

Harald's eyes sparkled, but he was suspicious. "What do you mean?"

"A simple wager. My village versus yours. Whoever gets the most points tomorrow wins."

"This had better not be another trick."

Magnus opened out his hands. "Honest, no tricks. You do want to win your shield back, don't you?" Magnus stood the shield in front of him and rested his elbow on it.

"What's in it for you, Bone-Breaker?"

"Oh, that's the fun bit. If I win I get your sword, Whirlwind."

Erik the Ear-Masher, Harald's second in command, interrupted: "No, you can't do it!"

"He's right," said Oswald. "The sword and shield

are the symbols of your power as village chief. If he wins he'll have both, and you know what that means."

"Magnus will be our chief, not you!" said Erik.

"So that's it," said Harald. "You want to take over my village?"

Magnus shrugged and rested his head on his hand. "That, and also it's a matching set. I hate to break them up."

Harald's eyes twitched. He stepped up close to Magnus. They were almost nose-to-nose. "I'll take your wager," he snarled.

Magnus clapped his hands together. "Excellent! So tomorrow we will see!" He turned away, laughing.

Erik stepped up to Harald's side. "You idiot! Why did you accept? It's bound to be a trick."

"What does it matter?" replied Harald. "We have the Thunder-Belly, Logrid and Floki; they are more than a match for anyone in Magnus's village. As long as we have them, we can win the bet.

CHAPTER 9

The following morning Velda woke to the sound of groaning coming from outside. It sounded like a walrus with its moustache caught in a crab's nippers.

"OW... OW... OW... OW."

She banged the roof of her bunk, waking Thorfinn, who was in the one above. "Did you hear that?"

Thorfinn poked his head down over the edge, listening. "Why yes, old friend."

"Hear what?" cried Oswald from the top bunk.

"I can't hear anything for that awful moaning."

Thorfinn and Velda jumped down from their bunks and threw open the door.

"Wait for me, you fools!" cried Oswald. His bottom was already sticking out of the bunk. One of his legs was dangling below, his toe seeking out the rung of the ladder. But they were already gone. "Eh ... help! I'm stuck."

"OW... OW... OW... OW."

The noise was coming from the next hut.

The two children burst in to find Hagar lying on the bottom bunk, clutching his stomach.

"Whatever is the matter, Mr Thunder-Belly?" asked Thorfinn.

Hagar grimaced and pointed to the barrel of oysters next to his bed.

"Someone... someone's poisoned my oysters. I can't belch today," said Hagar.

"Oh dear!" said Thorfinn.

The two children raced towards Harald's hut. Their way was blocked by two men carrying a stretcher.

"ow ... ow ... ow ... ow."

It was Floki. He was nursing a badly bruised shoulder.

"Mr Sea-Urchin, what happened?" asked Thorfinn.

"I dived into the shallow lake," replied Floki.

There were two lakes on the island. Only one of them was deep enough for swimming.

"But they're both signposted," said Velda.

"Someone must have switched the signs. Tell the chief I'm sorry, I can't swim today." Floki groaned as the men carried him away.

They found Harald slumped by the smouldering remains of the campfire, his head in his hands. He already knew about Floki, and he wasn't surprised to hear about Hagar. "And Logrid too! What are we going to do?"

"Logrid the Limb-Splitter, our axe thrower? What happened to him?" asked Thorfinn.

"Someone bashed him on the head when he got up during the night to go to the toilet," said Harald.

"Oh dear, is he alright?"

"There's good news and bad news. The good news is he's up and about and talking."

"And the bad news?"

"He's got concussion and thinks he's a horse." Harald pointed at the long line of horses standing by the fence, with their noses in a trough. At the end of the line stood Logrid, his nose also in a trough.

"Mmmm. Oats, good oats," said Logrid. They went over to see him.

"Dearest Mr Limb-Splitter," said Thorfinn, "wouldn't you like to sit down for five minutes?"

Suddenly one of the horses bolted into the field, and the others followed. "Hey, wait for me! NEIGH!" Logrid cried, cantering across the field.

"Pull yourself together! You're a man, not a horse!" Harald shouted after him.

"I don't think he'll be doing much axe throwing today, do you?" said Velda.

* * *

Back at the campfire, trouble was brewing.

Magnus the Bone-Breaker had turned up, flanked
by his men and his enormous son. He had a huge
smug grin on his face.

The purple-robed games steward, Sir Fergus, was
also there, carrying a big book marked **RULES**.

Harald was furious. "Magnus is to blame. He's
been taking out all my star players."

Magnus let out a gasp of astonishment so fake
that even the actors would have been impressed.
"Are you accusing me?"

"You're a liar!" cried Harald.

"What proof do you have, eh? It's just bad luck,
that's all." Magnus folded his arms, and looked even

more smug. "Of course, now you don't have enough competitors to win the bet."

"Aha! So that's your game, eh?" cried Harald. "Well, I'll compete in all the contests myself. I can throw an axe, belch and swim better than anyone."

Magnus wagged his finger. "Ah, I don't think so. You're already down for sword fighting. According to the rules, the same man cannot compete in more than one contest." He turned to Sir Fergus. "Isn't that right?"

"I'm afraid so," said the steward. "Rules are rules."

"And you don't have anyone to spare, do you?" smirked Magnus.

Harald looked around his men. Each and every one of them had signed up for something. There was Leif the Tonsil-Impaler, but he was down for the pie-clobbering competition. Then there was Knut the Nun-Slinger, but he was down for wild-boar teasing. Even the cook was signed up. He was quite good at goat throwing.

No one.

Harald sunk to the ground. "I don't believe it."

"Yes," said Magnus, proudly admiring his fingernails. "And you know what that means, don't you?"

It meant they were about to get a new chief.

"H-H-H-H-O-OOLLLD on there!" said Oswald the wise man, sounding like a camel with a tickle in its throat. He was still wearing his nightshirt and was nursing a large bruise on his forehead.

He jabbed his cane at Magnus, and placed

his hands on Thorfinn and Velda's shoulders. "We do have competitors. Velda can throw an axe. Thorfinn is a very capable swimmer. And I was known to belch quite magnificently in my youth."

"What, you three? Are you joking?" Magnus and his men burst out laughing. "I've never heard

anything so funny in all my life." They started falling about and pointing.

That was, until Harald whipped out his sword, raised it high over his head, and brought it down with a mighty roar onto a bench. The bench split in two and somersaulted into the air, crashing down around them. He glared at Magnus and his men, his eye twitching menacingly.

"You'll be laughing on the other side of your faces in a bit," said Harald. "Because the bet is still on, and thanks to these three WE ARE GOING TO WIN!"

CHAPTER 10

An hour later, the Vikings flung open the gates of
their stockade and marched out. Their helmets,
swords and belt buckles were polished and
gleaming. Led by men blowing battle
horns, they trooped down to the
games area at the centre of the
island. Velda and Thorfinn
walked alongside Oswald,
who had decided to put
Logrid to use as a horse
and was riding on his back.

"Onward, my brave steed!" cried Oswald.

"NEIGH!" cried Logrid.

The other stockades opened too, and out marched the tribes representing the other peoples of the west. There were the Angles, a proud, wealthy and civilised race. There were the Scots, wearing tartan and led by pipers. There were the Britons, who all had moustaches and wore plaid trousers.

Some were driving brightly painted chariots. And finally there were the Picts, a wild people whose language no one else could understand. They always seemed to be fighting each other. Their faces were painted blue and their bodies were covered in tattoos.

All the tribes assembled around the games area.

Then a man on the battlements of the fort blew a giant horn, signalling the start of the Gruesome Games. With that, the day's competitions began.

The day began well for Harald's team. Erik the Ear-Masher won the hammer-tossing contest, while Harald himself won at sword fighting. They were already ahead of Magnus's team in points.

Oswald's belching event was held in a large hollow in the ground.

"It helps to amplify the belching sounds," explained Thorfinn, as he and Velda squeezed into a seat among the spectators on the bank.

The competitors were lined up in the centre of the amphitheatre. Each of them had their very own technique for producing the finest burp. One of them used pickled herring, another used his granny's lentil soup, and a third used extra frothy ale. The crowd applauded and cheered.

At last it was Oswald's turn. He stepped onto the stage carrying a bucket. He put it down, then dunked his hand in and pulled out a tiny live fish. He held it in the air for a moment for all to see, and then popped it in his mouth.

"Yuck!" said Velda.

"The fish swims about and stirs up the stomach gases," explained Thorfinn.

Oswald stood for a second in silence, his hands clasped behind his back. The hubbub grew as the spectators waited for something to happen.

Oswald held up a single finger, then a look of concentration came across his face. He leaned back, opened his mouth, and...

BUUUUUURRRRP

The crowd applauded, surprised by how good a belch it was.

"Go Oswald!" cried Velda.

Oswald bowed to the crowd, coughed up the fish, held it in the air for all to see again – it was still alive! – and then popped it back into the bucket.

And sure enough, it kept them ahead of Magnus's team.

✳ ✳ ✳

Next it was Velda and the axe-throwing competition. Her first contest was against Fritz the Angle, who, like Logrid, was tall and skinny, with long arms for throwing. As Velda stepped onto the green by the castle, the crowd laughed.

"Such a small girl," they said.

"Such skinny arms."

"Is this a joke?"

But Velda paid them no attention. She stepped up to the mark and bowed to her opponent. Then she spat into her hands and picked up her axe.

It was quite something to see a very small girl throwing a very large axe. She span faster and faster on the spot, before finally letting it go with

an ear-splitting yell.
The axe didn't just
hit the target – it hit the
bull's-eye! The crowd
erupted. No one had seen
anything like it. Neither had
the other competitors, who all
crowded round her, demanding
to know where she'd learnt her
throwing style.

"Who taught you? Was it Philippe the Axe Master
of Paris?"

"The screaming Earl of Munster?"

"Ethel the Lady Knight of Basingstoke? Tell us!"

Velda shrugged them all off and headed straight

for Thorfinn and Oswald, who had been watching from the sidelines.

"Quite brilliant, old friend!" said Thorfinn.

"A great showing!" cried Oswald. "Logrid would be proud of you. If he didn't think he was a horse."

"NEIGH!" said Logrid, who was standing behind them, munching hay.

Velda managed to get through two heats before she was knocked out in the quarter-finals. Unfortunately Magnus's man, Argrid the Door-Chopper-Downer, made it to the semi-finals, which put Harald's team behind on points.

By the afternoon, attention turned to the swimming lake. It was Thorfinn's turn.

CHAPTER 11

Thorfinn got through his heat easily. His opponent in the semi-final was a Pict whose name no one could pronounce, though someone said it sounded like a sheep being tickled to death. He fell asleep halfway through swimming and had to be rescued. He claimed it was down to stomach flu but everyone knew the real reason: the Picts had been drinking too much honeyed mead, as they always did. Sometimes they even fell asleep halfway through battles.

The final was going to be very different though.

Velda, Oswald and Harald were among the crowd at the lakeside as Thorfinn stepped up next to his opponent.

"Come on, Thorfinn!" yelled Velda.

Magnus the Bone-Breaker sidled up to Harald with an unusually-smug-even-for-him look on his face.

"Of course, you do know who your son's opponent is, don't you?"

Harald nodded grimly. It was last year's Champion of Champions, the winner of the Gruesome Games, Brendan the Briton. He was tall, muscular and broad-shouldered, with a face like a cliff edge. Swimming was his speciality.

"He beat his opponent last year by drowning him – did you know that?" asked Magnus. "I dread to think what he's going to do to that teensy little boy of yours."

Harald bristled with anger, but he knew his opponent was right. Brendan the Briton was eyeing up Thorfinn like he was a morning snack.

Brendan growled at Thorfinn.

"You know what I'm going to do? I'm going to have you for breakfast."

"I beg your pardon, sir?" said Thorfinn.

"In fact, I'm going to have you for breakfast, lunch and dinner."

Thorfinn's face lit up. "How nice of you to offer to have me over for all that food. I should be delighted to meet you for breakfast tomorrow if convenient."

"Oh, smart guy, eh?" snarled Brendan. "Well, watch this!" He grabbed a piece of raw fish from a nearby basket. He bit into it and then noisily spat out the flesh. "See that, pipsqueak? That's what I do to all small sea creatures like you."

"What excellent teeth you have," said Thorfinn. "I would have cooked that fish first though. It's not very hygienic to eat it raw."

"Oh yeh? Oh yeh?" Brendan was getting annoyed that his taunts were being ignored. "Well tonight you are going to be SLEEPING with the fishes."

"Really?" Thorfinn scratched his head, puzzled. "I can't imagine sleeping in the lake will be very comfortable. But, I promised my father that I would

do everything I could to fit in, so I'm happy to try."

"READY! SET..." The steward blew his whistle.

Thorfinn dived neatly into the water, while Brendan dived not-so-neatly on top of Thorfinn.

Brendan made a grab for him, but Thorfinn wriggled out of the big man's clutches.

The crowd watched as Thorfinn swam to the other end of the lake, cutting through the water with ease. Compared to Thorfinn, Brendan was like a big floundering whale.

Thorfinn smiled and waved over at Velda and the rest. "Good day, one and all!" This brought a huge cheer from the crowd. Everyone loves an underdog.

As Brendan closed in on him, Thorfinn dipped under the water again. Brendan looked around, treading water.

Then Thorfinn's head appeared again, this time in the shallower end. Brendan was furious. He chased after him, thrashing through the water.

Thorfinn's head ducked under the water, but this time Brendan went under too.

The water was still, then after a moment there was lots of thrashing around just under the surface.

"Brendan must have caught him," said someone. "The boy is in for it now."

Harald broke out in a cold sweat, and felt terribly sick. What if something happened to his little son?

He could never forgive himself. He was about to
jump into the water, when suddenly the thrashing
stopped. Two heads appeared and began bobbing
towards the finishing point.

As they drew closer it became clear that Thorfinn
was dragging an unconscious Brendan the Briton
behind him.

There was shocked silence among the crowd,
and some men helped lift Brendan out of the water.
They laid him down and thumped him in the middle

of the chest. Brendan coughed up water, then came round slowly. "Urgh. What happened?"

"He'll be fine," said one of the men.

Thorfinn nodded, then he climbed out of the water and stood on the pier, smiling and looking with some puzzlement at the gawping faces around him. "My poor friend Brendan is indisposed. Would anyone care to join me for another swim?"

The crowd erupted. "All hail Thorfinn!" They started chanting his name over and over again.

"That's my son," cried Harald, proudly pointing him out. "That's my boy, you know."

The other Vikings picked Thorfinn up and carried him off towards camp. "How did you beat him, Thorfinn?" they asked. "Tell us your secret!"

CHAPTER 12

"Reeds," explained Thorfinn. "The poor man's leg got caught in the reeds, so all I did was dive down and free him. Did I do anything wrong?"

They were back at their camp sitting round the fire. The other Vikings were listening to Thorfinn's story. Now they all burst out laughing.

Erik the Ear-Masher shouldered his way through the crowd to Harald's side. "Did you hear the news? We've finished joint top of the leader board. Beating Brendan the Briton won us loads of points."

There was a ripple of excitement among those gathered round.

"What?! Joint top with who?" said Harald, hoping for a second that he'd beaten Magnus and won his shield back.

"Magnus of course."

"It's hardly a surprise," said Oswald. "Magnus cheated in almost every contest." It was true. Most of his competitors weren't from his village. In fact they weren't even Vikings. Magnus had hired them from all over Europe and beyond.

Harald breathed a huge sigh of relief. He hadn't lost the bet. The village was still his, and that was the most important thing.

"We must celebrate!" cried Harald, and they held a

great feast. They toasted Thorfinn, along with Velda and Oswald.

❉ ❉ ❉

It wasn't until the feast was dying down that Magnus showed up once again. He still looked smug, even though he hadn't won. Sir Fergus was at his side, cradling the rule book.

Magnus stretched out his hand to Harald. "Well, I just wanted to say well done. I don't know how you managed it, but you did."

Harald slapped Magnus's

hand away. "You rat! You weasel! You snake!"

Magnus shrugged. "Fair enough." He turned to go, but then stopped. "I don't suppose you'd be interested in one last challenge? The steward here says a fight often happens to settle a draw." Sir Fergus nodded.

Erik grabbed Harald by the shoulder. "Don't listen to him. It's another trick."

"We've had enough of your bets!" said Harald.

"That's a shame." Magnus took off the shield and rubbed the shiny bronzy bits with his finger. "I would have loved to give you a chance to win back Sword-Blunter."

Harald trembled with rage and gazed longingly down at his old shield.

Magnus continued: "A clean sword fight. Your champion versus mine."

Harald's eyes lit up. "A sword fight?"

"Have you lost your mind?" said Erik. "It's a trick."

"But what trick could there be?" asked Harald. "He said it himself. A straightforward sword fight." He jabbed himself in the chest with his thumb. "I'll pick myself. And I hope you pick yourself, Bone-Breaker. I'd love to get the chance to bash your bones in once and for all."

"Excellent!" Magnus turned to Sir Fergus. "Did you hear that? We're on." The steward nodded. Then Magnus turned back to Harald, grinning. "Though I'm afraid it won't be possible for you and me to meet."

"What?" asked Harald. "I'm the chief. I pick the

champion. That's how it works."

"Ah, but you're forgetting that games rules apply here." Magnus turned back to Sir Fergus. "Isn't that right?"

Sir Fergus opened his book. "The rules are clear. In matters of single combat to decide the Champion of Champions, the trial is to be contested between the two competitors on each side with the most points."

"So who is my champion?"

The smuggest possible grin spread across Magnus's face as he turned his eye on Thorfinn.

"WHAT?!" cried Harald.

"He defeated Brendan the Briton, the defending Champion of Champions," said Sir Fergus. "That gave him more points than any other competitor."

"And who's your highest point scorer?" asked Harald.

Magnus beckoned with his finger. Out of the crowd stepped his enormous, gloomy-faced son, Osric the Brick-Swallower, winner of the elk-lifting competition.

CHAPTER 13

After Magnus and his men left, Harald led Thorfinn,
along with Velda and Oswald, away from the fire to
the quietest part of the camp. They sat down among
beer barrels and chickens hanging upside down,
plucked and ready for the pot.

"Look, Thorfinn, do you understand what is going
to happen tomorrow?" said Harald.

"Er, yes," said Thorfinn, trying to be polite, then he
shook his head. "No, not really. But it sounds fun."

"No, Thorfinn. You're going to be up against a
very big, powerful boy. Unless we can turn you into

a ferocious maniac by morning then the big boy is going to win."

Velda was incensed. "But then we'll have Magnus for a chief!"

"Fat lot of good you were," said Harald to Velda. "You were supposed to be training him to be angry."

"Yes, and I've had an idea about that. Stay right there!" Velda got up and ran off in the direction of the fire. Then she returned leading one of the actors.

Thorfinn stood up to greet him. "Good evening, sir. It's a pleasure to meet you. I'm a great admirer."

"This man," said Velda, "is going to teach you the tricks of his trade. Which means that tomorrow the world is going to see a whole new Thorfinn."

"What are you on about, girl?" said Harald.

"Look, I can't make Thorfinn angry. But I *can* make him *seem* angry."

Oswald was sitting lopsided on a giant sack of turnips. "Whatever you do," he said, straining his eyes in the darkness, "be true to yourself, for then you cannot be false with anyone." Unfortunately he wasn't addressing Thorfinn, but one of the upside-down chickens.

"Hmm, wise words for any chicken, old friend," said Thorfinn.

Later, Harald went to bed worried. They couldn't pull out of the big fight tomorrow. The honour of the village would be lost. But what about his little boy – gentle, kind Thorfinn? How could the nicest Viking charm his way out of this one?

CHAPTER 14

The following morning, all the different tribes on the island assembled on the plain by the castle.

Magnus and his son Osric, who was dressed for battle, stepped into the middle and waited. But where was Thorfinn?

"Ha!" cried Magnus. "He's run away! I knew it. Harald forfeits the bet."

He spoke too soon: a tiny figure stepped out from the crowd. He was wielding a sword and shield and wearing armour.

"That's Thorfinn!" said someone in the crowd.

"He beat Brendan the Briton!" said someone else.

"They say his very name strikes terror into men's hearts," said another.

"Let combat begin!" cried Sir Fergus.

Thorfinn roared, then charged the field, screaming and waving his sword around.

It was a performance that would make any actor proud. This sent a ripple of excitement through the crowd.

Osric the Brick-Swallower didn't move. He just stood there, watching with a puzzled expression, his sword hanging at his side.

Thorfinn ran right up to him, then stopped. He took off his helmet. "Good day, my dear sir!"

Osric nodded. "Uh, good day. No, wait. I'm supposed to be hitting you."

"I'm supposed to be acting. Take that!" Thorfinn waved his sword around again.

Osric looked over at his dad, who mimed vicious punching. Osric gave a sad sigh. "OK, c'mere." And he grabbed at Thorfinn.

"Oh, a chasing game," said Thorfinn. "I LOVE chasing."

Osric chased Thorfinn round and round in circles until he got tired, and jeers and boos went up from the crowd.

"Stand still so I can thump you and get this over with!" said Osric.

"Thump me? Why would you want to do that?"

Osric slumped down onto the ground, panting. "I don't know. I don't like hitting people. My dad told me to. He says I'm a monster. Maybe I am."

"A monster? No, you look like a jolly nice fellow to me."

"Do I really?" said Osric. "Dad's always getting me to beat people up. I hate it. I'd rather stay at home. I have a pet tortoise called Gar."

"I have a pet pigeon," said Thorfinn. On cue Percy fluttered out of the sky and landed on his shoulder. "He's called Percy."

"That's a nice pigeon."

The jeers and boos from the crowd were getting louder.

"What are you doing, boring him to death?"

someone yelled.

"Hit him, you idiot!" yelled Magnus.

Osric huffed. "He's always calling me that."

"You know," said Thorfinn, "my dear old friend,

Oswald, said just last night that you must be true to

yourself, for then you can't be false to anyone."

Osric thought about this, rubbing his chin. "Hmm, I'm not sure I understand what it means, but I like it anyway."

Thorfinn plonked himself down next to Osric. "What do you really want to do?"

"Me and my pals, we have a band. It's called Rune Direction. I play the drums."

"You're too good at fighting; that's the problem. You keep winning."

Osric looked over at his father, who was jumping up and down and turning red.

"You're right," said Osric. "There's only one thing for it. I'll have to lose."

"Did you ever hear the story of the great

Gruesome Games sword fight?" asked Thorfinn.

"The one with the Pictish knight fighting the common sailor? Of course! Everyone has heard that one."

"I have an idea. Why don't we act it out for them? Without any burying on the beach. It'll be fun. I do love acting."

"That's a great idea!" said Osric. "But remember: you have to win at the end."

Thorfinn and Osric stood up, faced each other as if they were deadly foes, and began sword fighting.

"At last! Now we're getting somewhere!" cried Magnus.

The two boys fought for hours. Their fight carried them right across the island, up hills and over clifftops, just like in the old legend. The crowd followed them, cheering them on and placing bets.

"Where did Thorfinn learn to fight like that?"
yelled Erik.

"He didn't," said Harald.

"He just learnt to *act* like that," said Velda.

The five great tribes of the games seemed to
forget their differences as the fight wore on. They
knew they were seeing something special: a new
great legend. Scots, Picts, Angles, Vikings and Britons
now stood shoulder to shoulder as they watched.

Finally the two boys arrived back where they'd started.

"I'll fall down and pretend to be knocked out," said Osric.

"Righto, dear pal."

Osric stumbled dramatically to the ground and lay still.

Which is how Thorfinn the Very-Very-Nice-Indeed ended up standing over Osric the Brick-Swallower and being declared the winner of the Gruesome Games.

Osric made an amazingly swift recovery. He leapt up to shake Thorfinn's hand. "Well done, friend, and thank you," he said.

Then Brendan the Briton, the swimmer, stepped up. "Well done, Thorfinn. Thank you for saving my life."

Then Velda ran onto the field, swinging her axe and shouting, "Yay Thorfinn!"

And Oswald, who was still riding Logrid like a horse, said, "Well done, young friend!"

"NEIGH!" cried Logrid.

Harald stepped towards Magnus. "Now, give me back my shield, Bone-Breaker."

Magnus flung the shield at Harald, and muttered, "I'll get you back for this, Skull-Splitter. You'll see." He grabbed Osric by the collar and turned to leave, but

Osric pushed his father away and returned to the happy celebrations.

Harald addressed his tribe. "At last, my sword and shield are together once more." Then he turned to Thorfinn and tapped the boy's cheek. "And, more importantly, my boy has come out winning again."

The crowd of Vikings, Angles, Scots, Britons and Picts picked Thorfinn up and carried him towards the platform in the middle of the plain. They put him down at Sir Fergus's feet. The steward bowed.

"The Great Hammer is yours, champion." He stepped away, to reveal the hammer gleaming in the sunlight.

"Why, thank you, sir." Thorfinn walked around it, stroking his chin. Up close it was very large indeed. Larger than him in fact. "But how am I to lift such a thing?"

The crowd laughed, and Harald stepped forward and placed a hand on Thorfinn's shoulder. "Don't worry, my boy. I'll carry it for you."

"**HUZZAH!**" the crowd cheered.

Harald shouted over them with his huge booming voice: "All hail Thorfinn the Very-Very-Nice-Indeed, Champion of the Gruesome Games!"

RICHARD THE PICTURE-CONQUEROR

DAVID THE STORY-CHIEF

DAVID MACPHAIL left home at eighteen to travel the world and have adventures. After working as a chicken wrangler, a ghost-tour guide and a waiter on a tropical island, he now has the sensible job of writing about yetis and Vikings. At home in Perthshire, Scotland, he exists on a diet of cream buns and zombie movies.

RICHARD MORGAN was born and raised by goblins on the Yorkshire moors. After running away to New Zealand to play with yachts and paint backgrounds for Disney TV he returned to the UK to write and illustrate children's books. He now lives in Cambridge, England, and has a family of goblins of his own.

GRUESOME GAMES
SCROLL ⊕F WINNERS

AXE THROWING	Edmund of Northumbria (Angle)
BEAR STARING	Mungo the Goggly-Eyed (Scot)
BELCHING	Drest the Gaseous (Pict)
ELK LIFTING	Osric the Brick-Swallower (Viking)
GARLIC EATING	Guy the Friendless (Angle)
GOAT THROWING	Sven the Ruminant-Chucker (Viking)
HAMMER TOSSING	Erik the Ear-Masher (Viking)
HORSE VAULTING	Neville the Springy (Briton)
MACHETE DODGING	Ulric the Armless (Viking)
PIE CLOBBERING	Greg the Messy-Faced of Dalriada (Scot)
SPEAR TICKLING	Knut the Nimble-Footed (Briton)
SWIMMING	Thorfinn the Very-Very-Nice-Indeed (Viking)
SWORD FIGHTING	Harald the Skull-Splitter (Viking)
TURF SLINGING	Nechtan the Grassy-Headed (Pict)
WIFE CATAPULTING	Senga of Ballachulish (Scot)*
WILD-BOAR TEASING	Wilbur the Very-Bruised of Yorkshire (Angle)

*Won by one of the wives after she rebelled and insisted on catapulting her husband instead.

VIKING WORDSEARCH

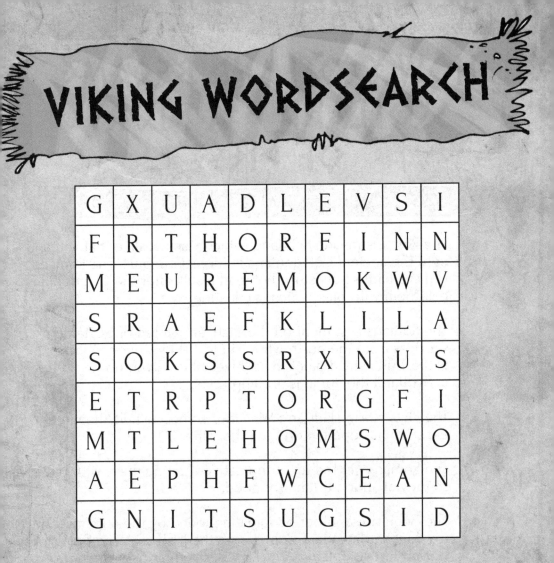

G	X	U	A	D	L	E	V	S	I
F	R	T	H	O	R	F	I	N	N
M	E	U	R	E	M	O	K	W	V
S	R	A	E	F	K	L	I	L	A
S	O	K	S	S	R	X	N	U	S
E	T	R	P	T	O	R	G	F	I
M	T	L	E	H	O	M	S	W	O
A	E	P	H	F	W	C	E	A	N
G	N	I	T	S	U	G	S	I	D

VIKINGS   SCOTS   GAMES

DISGUSTING   AWFUL   THORFINN

FEAST   INVASION   VELDA

ROTTEN   GRUESOME

HOW SCOTLAND BECAME SCOTLAND – A STORY OF PIES*

84 AD
The Romans invade Scotland (which wasn't called that yet) and fight the ancient Caledonians at Mons Graupius. The Romans win the battle, but return home in a sulk after the Caledonians pelt them with pies, which is cheating.

297 AD
The Romans first mention the 'Picti' or painted ones, fierce warriors from the north who eat pies. They wear no clothes in battle, but instead paint themselves blue. Given how cold it is in Scotland the Romans are impressed.

367 AD
The Picts storm Hadrian's Wall after someone tells them a new pie shop has opened on the other side.

410 AD
The Romans get fed up of the natives pelting them with pies, so they abandon Britain for good.

500 AD
The 'Scoti' are another people mentioned by the Romans. The word means 'invaders from across the Irish sea'. The Scots (or Gaels) start colonising Argyll. They call their new kingdom Dalriada. They soon develop a taste for pies.

550 AD
King Arthur and Merlin visit the Britons' capital at Dumbarton, where they feast on pies. Later, King Arthur builds a big round table in the shape of an enormous pie.

638 AD
Angles from Northumbria capture Edinburgh and close all the pie shops.

685 AD The Picts defeat the Angles at the Battle of Nechtansmere and reopen all the pie shops. Hurrah!

795 AD The Vikings begin raiding Scotland and colonising the Northern Isles. They try the pies but wonder what all the fuss is about.

840 AD King Kenneth MacAlpine unites Pictland and Dalriada. Scotland is born. He declares free pies for everyone!

VIKINGS

PICTS

SCOTS

URAIG ISLAND

BRITONS

ANGLES

*These facts are mostly true, apart from the bit about the pies.

PERCY THE PIGEON POST

EST. 799AD   THORSDAY 23RD JUNE   PRICE: ONE EARLO

SKULL-SPLITTING NEWS

In what will forever be known as the **Awful Invasion** the Scots have narrowly missed being invaded by a band of maurauding Vikings, led by the fearsome Chief of Indgar, Harald the Skull-Splitter. "His son, Thorfinn the Very-Very-Nice-Indeed, is his only weak spot," confided an anonymous source with disturbing ears.

SPORTING HEADLINES

It is the weekend of the annual **Gruesome Games**. Word on the beach is that Thorfinn the Very-Very-Nice-Indeed, wise-man Oswald and (hold on to your axes), Velda – a GIRL – must save their village from the clutches of Magnus the Bone-Breaker. Odds are on for a new Chief of Indgar by Monday.

TORTUROUS TRAVEL

If you happen to b kidnapped by the **Rotte Scots** and held at Cast Mad Dog, you'll fin plenty of activities fo friendly non-Viking such as sewing and fishing All under the caref instruction of its mos famous captive, Thorfin the Very-Very-Nice-Indeed

Early booking essentia for he may be 'rescued' a any moment.

FOULSOME FOOD

It's all about Le Poisson (that's FISH to you boneheads). The King of Norway is on his way to Indgar and he expects a most **Disgusting Feast**. Can Thorfinn the Very-Very-Nice-Indeed organise a banquet of beasts? With a poisoner at large? The heat is on in the kitchen...